# SUPER ME

## Stephanie Conquers Hate

By

Sydney Elise Russell

**Super ME**

Copyright © 2022 Sydney Elise Russell

Contact:
Sydney@successteam1.com
Visit: www.SydneyElise.com

ISBN: 979-8-9863631-0-3

Printed in the United States of America

Stephanie woke up to the smell of pancakes, and that could only mean one thing...it was Saturday morning!

Every Saturday, Stephanie's dad made his famous pancakes. She looked forward to this special breakfast treat every weekend.

After putting on her slippers, Stephanie went downstairs for breakfast.

"Hi, Daddy!"

"Good Morning, Baby Girl! I hope you're ready for pancakes!"

"You know it!"

"Don't start without me!" her mother exclaimed as she walked into the kitchen.

They sat down together and enjoyed the delicious breakfast.

After breakfast, Stephanie got dressed.  She took her magical bracelet out of her desk drawer and placed it on her wrist.  Ever since receiving the bracelet from Fairy Princess Jessica and fighting the Beety Bug Monster, she wore it every day.

"You never know when you'll need to fight another monster," Stephanie said to herself.

"You're exactly right!" a voice suddenly exclaimed.

Stephanie whirled around and was startled to see Jessica.

"Fairy Princess Jessica, what are YOU doing here?"

"Official business!"  Jessica responded with a smile. "I'm here to collect the stone of the Beety Bug Monster!  Did I mention I'm proud of you?"

Stephanie smiled brightly and took the pink stone from her desk drawer.  As she placed the stone in Jessica's hand, she proudly remembered the day she had overcome fear by bravely destroying the Beety Bug Monster.

"Stephanie, I'm also here to give you a warning.  The second monster, the Smashing Bird, has been hovering around Earth.  Be sure to guard your heart against hate, and be prepared to fight him, if necessary."

"I will," Stephanie replied confidently. Inside, she hoped today would be a monster-free day.

"That's all for now.  I know you can do it!"

Jessica's image faded as she waved goodbye.

As Stephanie thought about the Smashing Bird, she looked out from her bedroom window and saw her friend Chloe jumping rope outside.

She grabbed her jump rope from her closet and ran downstairs to ask for permission to join her friend.  Her parents were watching television in the family room.

"Mom and Dad, can I go outside and jump rope with Chloe?"

"Chloe from next door?" Her mother asked.  Stephanie nodded.

"Sure, that's fine." Her father replied.

"Just stay in front of our house," her mother added.

"Thank you," said Stephanie, "I promise I will!"  She headed outside to meet up with Chloe.

Chloe greeted her warmly, "Hi Stephanie!  Happy Saturday!"

The girls chatted and jumped rope together for a while, then they saw someone on a bicycle riding up the street.

It was Alan, a boy who lived three houses away from Stephanie.

"Oh no!  Here comes Alan.  All he does is talk about dinosaurs.  He's so... strange," said Chloe.

"Hi guys!  What are you up to?" Alan asked.

"Just jumping rope," said Stephanie, "Do you want to join us?"

"I can try!  Hey, did you know the Tyrannosaurus Rex was a carnivore with razor sharp teeth?"

"I told you.  Dinosaurs!" Chloe said with a frown.

"What's wrong with dinosaurs?" asked Alan

"I hate dinosaurs, and since that's all you ever talk about, **I hate you too!**" Chloe yelled.

Stephanie couldn't believe what her friend had said.  Alan's eyes filled with sadness, but before Stephanie could say anything a loud, squawking noise echoed through the air.

Stephanie looked up to see a large bird with enormous wings flying overhead.  She remembered Jessica's warning.

*"This must be the Smashing Bird,"* she thought.

Chloe's hatred toward Alan had drawn the monster right to them. Stephanie had no idea what the bird would try to do, but she knew she had to protect herself and her friends.

The monster squawked again and flew directly at Stephanie. Its massive wings sliced through the air with ease. She had to think fast!

She thought of a quote by Dr. Martin Luther King, Jr., which her mother and father had taught her, about fighting hate. She recalled each word and felt her confidence grow.

Her bracelet glowed on her wrist, and suddenly, she was wearing her superhero outfit!

Stephanie planted her feet as the Smashing Bird swooped down over her. She stretched out her hands and yelled, "Hate cannot drive out hate, only **LOVE** can do that! Love lives here!"

Each of her words pierced the air, and beams of light engulfed the Smashing Bird. The monster screeched in terror, burst into a bright flame, and disappeared.

Stephanie stared at the sky with a mix of disbelief and pride.

On the ground near her feet, a note and an orange stone suddenly appeared.  Stephanie defeated the Smashing Bird and collected a new stone!

The note simply read, "You did it again!  Keep the stone in a safe place, and I'll see you soon!"

Stephanie smiled and turned to see her friends looking at her curiously. She quickly slipped the stone and note in her pants pocket.  Her superhero outfit had vanished.

"Stephanie, are you okay?"  "Why were you yelling?" Alan asked.

"*Wow!*" Stephanie thought, "*They must not have seen anything!*"

"Oh, you know me, just being funny!"

Stephanie took a deep breath, "Chloe, you need to apologize to Alan. It's not right to hate someone because they're different from you.  I know you wouldn't want someone to treat you that way."

Chloe thought for a second, realizing Stephanie was right. "Alan, I'm sorry I was mean to you. Can we be friends?"

Alan smiled, "Sure! I forgive you. I have lots more to tell you about dinosaurs too!"

Chloe laughed, "Okay, I'm all ears!"

This was great! Stephanie conquered the Smashing Bird and helped Chloe and Alan get along too. They decided to meet up again the next day after church.

Stephanie walked back into the house.

"Did you have fun with Chloe?" Her father asked.

"Yes! We made a new friend too. Chloe didn't like him at first, but I convinced her to give him a chance."

"Great job, Baby Girl! Always lead with love because…"

Stephanie hugged her father as she finished his sentence, "Love conquers hate!"

# Journaling Reflection

Making new friends can be a lot of fun!  Often, you'll find you have lots in common. You're also able to learn about each other's differences.  Take a few minutes to journal about your experience with making new friends.

Feel free to use your own journal.

1.  Write about a time when you made a new friend.

   _____

   _____

2.  What did you discover you both had in common? What differences did you find?

   _____

   _____

3. How did it feel to learn about your new friend?

   _____

   _____

# About the Author

**Sydney Elise Russell** is an actress, author, singer, and dancer, who desires to share unique and inspiring stories with the world. Sydney became a first-time author in 2020 after publishing the first book in the Super ME Book Series, *Super ME: Stephanie and the Magical Bracelet.* As an actress, Sydney has an extensive performance resume. She helped to reopen Broadway in 2021, playing the role of Young Nala in Disney's The Lion King. Sydney is an avid crafter and resides in Richmond, TX with her family.

Visit SydneyElise.com to stay connected with Sydney and receive news and updates on her latest endeavors!

Made in the USA
Columbia, SC
11 December 2022

73474775R00018